CLUMSY CLARISSA

by TONY GARTH

Clarissa was a very clumsy little girl.

She was always bumping into things. Or knocking things over and breaking them. The trouble was that she never bothered to look where she was going.

"Oh not again, Clarissa!" scolded her Dad, when she got a potty stuck on her head. "You really must be more careful. If you looked where you were going, you'd not be so clumsy."

Clarissa thought long and hard about this. But it made no difference.

One day, she tripped over her tennis racket and bumped her head. She had to go to the hospital. Again! And she got another telling off from her Dad.

It made Clarissa very fed up. She decided to make one last, extra-big effort and to try not to be clumsy ever again.

First, she put her tennis racket away in her bedroom cupboard. There wasn't much room. The cupboard was crammed full of toys, books and all kinds of junk. She just about squeezed the racket in and quickly shut the door.

Stepping back, she nearly fell over a roller skate.

"Oops," she said. "That was close." And she opened the cupboard and threw the skate in.

Clarissa went into the living room. And nearly bumped into a spider dangling from the ceiling. The spider made her jump. She knocked over the coffee table and just managed to catch the vase of flowers before it smashed on the floor.

"Phew!" said Clarissa. "That was close, too." She picked up the spider and put it outside. She couldn't risk another fright. Then she picked up the vase of flowers. It was her mother's favourite. There was only one thing to do, to keep it safe...

She took the vase up to her bedroom and put it in her cupboard. And just to be extra specially sure, she squeezed the coffee table in too.

"Now I can't knock it over again," she thought.

Clarissa went outside to find her Dad.

On the way, she nearly stepped on a garden rake. But she managed to stop herself just in time.

"Phew!" she said again. "That was lucky."

And without further ado, she picked up the rake, went back indoors and put it away in her cupboard.

She went into the kitchen for a drink. And promptly tripped over the vacuum cleaner.

There was nothing else for it. The vacuum cleaner had to go straight into Clarissa's cupboard. Along with the teapot, the garden hose and the magazine rack. They were much too dangerous to leave lying about.

That evening, when Clarissa was having her bath, her Mum called up to her. "Clarissa," she said. "Where is the teapot?"

"Safe and sound," replied Clarissa. "I'll fetch it in a minute."

Next her Dad had a question.

"Clarissa," he called. "Have you seen the vacuum cleaner?"

"It's perfectly safe," Clarissa replied. "I'll fetch it in a minute."

She climbed very carefully out of the bath and put on her dressing gown.

"Clarissa, where on earth is the coffee table?" called her Dad. His voice was coming from her bedroom. "And the vase of flowers has gone missing too!"

Clarissa ran into her room. Just in time to see her Dad...opening the cupboard door.

"Oh no!" she shouted. "Don't open the..."

But it was too late! Her Dad opened the door and everything in the cupboard came crashing out around him. The vase of flowers hit him on the head and the spout and handle broke off the teapot. It was all a terrible mess.

Clarissa's Mum couldn't believe her eyes.

"Who's clumsy now?" she said to Clarissa's Dad.
Then she, Clarissa and her Dad all began to laugh.

"I'll help you clear up," said Clarissa and promptly
tripped over her Dad, straight into the cupboard.

Collect all 30 titles in the Little Monsters series

Printed in Scotland by Waddies Print Group. Tel: 01506 419393.